# Respecting the Contributions of
# Latino Americans

**Anna Kingston**

**PowerKiDS** press™

New York

Published in 2013 by The Rosen Publishing Group, Inc.
29 East 21st Street, New York, NY 10010

First Edition

Editor: Jennifer Way
Book Design: Erica Clendening and Ashley Drago
Layout Design: Andrew Povolny

Photo Credits: Cover Jose Cabezas/AFP/Getty Images; p. 4 Andy Dean Photography/Shutterstock.com; pp. 5, 11, 18 Alex Wong/Getty Images; p. 6 Rob Marmion/Shutterstock.com; p. 7 O Driscoll Imaging/Shutterstock.com; p. 10 New York Daily News Archive/Getty Images; p. 12 Peter Stackpole/Time & Life Pictures/Getty Images; p. 13 Hulton Archive/Archive Photos/Getty Images; p. 14 Cathy Murphy/Hulton Archive/Getty Images; p. 15 Mark Wilson/Getty Images; p. 16 Mark Ralston/AFP/Getty Images; p. 17 David McNew/Getty Images; p. 19 Kris Connor/Getty Images; p. 20 Michael Tran/FilmMagic/Getty Images; p. 21 David Redfern/Redferns/Getty Images; p. 22 Ron Levine/DIgital Vision/Getty Images.

Library of Congress Cataloging-in-Publication Data

Kingston, Anna.
Respecting the contributions of Latino Americans / by Anna Kingston. — 1st ed.
    p. cm. — (Stop bullying now!)
Includes index.
ISBN 978-1-4488-7449-1 (library binding) — ISBN 978-1-4488-7522-1 (pbk.) — ISBN 978-1-4488-7596-2 (6-pack)
1. Hispanic Americans—History–Juvenile literature. I. Title.
E184.S75K56 2013
973'.0468–dc23
                        2012006277

Manufactured in the United States of America

CPSIA Compliance Information: Batch #SW12PK: For Further Information contact Rosen Publishing, New York, New York at 1-800-237-9932

# Contents

# Roots in a Rich Culture

The United States is home to people of many races, religions, and **cultures**. Latino Americans are Americans who have roots in Latin American cultures. These cultures draw on the **traditions** of both Native Americans and people from Spain who settled in North or South America.

▲ Latino Americans are the largest minority group in the United States today.

US Secretary of the Interior Ken Salazar is Mexican American.

Latino Americans' roots can be in many countries. Baseball player David Ortiz is Dominican American, while actress Salma Hayek is Mexican American. From astronaut Ellen Ochoa, to scientists Luis Walter Alvarez and Mario Molina, to politicians Antonio Villaraigosa, Ken Salazar, and Marco Rubio, Latino Americans have made their marks in many fields.

Some Latino American kids face bullying. Bullies are people who hurt others. Some bullies hurt others physically. Other bullies say things that make other people feel upset, scared, or left out. Bullies who say these things online are called **cyberbullies**.

Bullies often target people who are different. For example, a bully might make fun of a girl who speaks English as her second language. A bully might also pick on a Latino

Cyberbullies may attack others using social networks, instant messages, or e-mails.

Most schools have a zero-tolerance policy for bullying. That means teachers and principals take reports of bullying seriously.

American boy because he eats different foods for lunch from what the bully eats. Bullying is wrong. Do not let others pull you into their bullying!

Some areas of today's United States were settled by Latino peoples before they became part of the United States. In 1821, the United States bought Florida from Spain. In 1836, Americans who had settled in the Southwest rebelled against Mexico and formed the Republic of Texas. Texas joined the United States in 1845. This set off the Mexican-American War. The United States won and took over land, including California, New Mexico, and Arizona.

In 1898, the United States and Spain fought over territories in the Americas in the Spanish-American War. The United States won and took over Puerto Rico and Cuba.

This map shows the territories the United States bought, took over, or won in wars between 1819 and 1898. ▶

# Spanish and Mexican Territory Taken Over by the United States

KEY

- Won in Mexican-American War in 1848
- Annexed from Mexico in 1845
- Purchased from Spain in 1819
- Won in Spanish-American War in 1898
- Gadsden Purchase from Mexico in 1853

# A Growing Population

While Puerto Rico became part of the United States in 1898, Cuba became a separate country in 1902. During the 1950s, many people from Puerto Rico moved to the US mainland to find jobs. In 1959, a revolution shook Cuba. Soon after, many Cubans

Big cities often have parades to honor the different countries from which people who live in the cities have come. This is a Dominican-American parade in New York City.

Florida senator Marco Rubio is a Cuban American whose parents emigrated from Cuba.

fled to the United States. In the years that followed, waves of people from the Dominican Republic, Central America, and South America **immigrated** to the United States.

The areas that were once part of Mexico already had a Mexican-American **population**. This grew throughout the twentieth century, as Mexicans came to the United States in search of jobs.

# Méndez v. Westminster

Though Latino Americans have a long history in the United States, they have often faced **discrimination** and other unfair treatment. Discrimination is treating someone differently because of his background. For example, school officials would not let the Mexican-American

California's Mexican-American schools were often poorly funded. In other parts of the Southwest, Latino Americans did not have to go to segregated schools but often lived in areas that were mostly Latino.

farmer Gonzalo Méndez sign his kids up to go to school in Westminster, California, in 1945. The officials said the kids had to go to a separate school for Mexican Americans.

Méndez and other parents went to court so their kids could go to school with everyone else. The judge ruled that this **segregation**, or separation based on background, was against the law.

Here, César Chávez speaks with a farmworker in a grape field in 1975. Chávez died in 1993.

Latino-American workers have often been treated unfairly. One leader who fought for workers' rights was César Chávez. He was born on March 31, 1927, near Yuma, Arizona. When he was 11, his family fell on hard times and lost their farm. They became **migrant workers**, or people who travel around to find work.

As an adult, Chávez became a **community organizer**. In 1962, he started the group that would become the United Farm Workers. He led events, such as marches and **strikes**. Strikes are when workers protest by not working. Chávez's efforts won better working conditions for many farmworkers.

Dolores Huerta cofounded the group that would become the United Farm Workers with César Chávez. She continues to be a labor leader and civil rights activist today.

# The Fight over Immigration

People from Latin America are the biggest group of immigrants arriving in the United States today. However, immigration laws limit the number of people who can enter the United States each year. Therefore, many immigrants, including some from Latin America, enter the United States **illegally**. Many illegal immigrants pay taxes and have lived in the United States for years.

These people are protesting Arizona's strict immigration law. They feel the law singles out Latinos to be stopped by police and asked to prove they are in the United States legally.

This is a naturalization ceremony for new American citizens.

Some people suspect that all Latino Americans are illegal immigrants. They view legal immigrants and Latino Americans who were born in the United States with distrust. Today, many Latino Americans are fighting to be treated fairly and to help illegal immigrants become legal ones.

# Latinos in Government

Latino Americans have found success in many fields, from the arts and sciences to business and government. In 2009, Sonia Sotomayor became

▲ Before a justice can join the Supreme Court, she must be approved by the US Senate. Here is Sotomayor during her Senate hearing before she joined the Supreme Court.

the first Latina, or Latino-American woman, to serve on the US Supreme Court. This is the country's highest court. Anything it decides is the law across the country.

Sotomayor was born in a part of New York City called the Bronx in 1954. Her family is from Puerto Rico. She did well in school and won **scholarships** to go to college and law school. She worked as a lawyer and a judge before joining the Supreme Court.

**Bill Richardson (1947–)**

Bill Richardson is another Latino American in government. Richardson's mother is Mexican, and he lived in Mexico until he was 13. He has served in Congress, as secretary of the Department of Energy, and as governor of New Mexico. Richardson was also the American ambassador to the United Nations.

# Making Music

Music is yet another field in which Latino Americans have found success. Latino cultures have produced many types of music. For example, merengue and bachata have roots in the Dominican Republic. Romeo Santos is a huge bachata

Jennifer Lopez is a world-famous singer, dancer, and actress. She is Puerto Rican.

star, while Olga Tañón is a popular merengue artist. Cuban and Puerto Rican traditions mixed together in the United States to create salsa. Reggaeton draws on the music of several Latino and Caribbean cultures.

Some Latino-American musicians, such as Jennifer Lopez and Ricky Martin, sing in English, too. They have become crossover stars, or popular outside of Latino-American communities.

## Tito Puente (1923–2000)

Tito Puente played a big role in the development of Latin music. Puente was born in New York City in 1923. His music drew from many traditions. It introduced lots of people to Latin music. He won many awards and is called the king of Latin music.

# A More Interesting Place

The United States is made up of people from many different backgrounds. However, some people think the country would be better off without Latino Americans. If you hear someone say this, stand up for your fellow Americans. Remind that person that the United States is a nation made up of immigrants from all over the world.

Everyone deserves respect. Share what you have learned to teach others about the important contributions of Latino Americans.

Understanding the history of different groups of Americans is an important part of learning to respect others.

# Glossary

**community organizer** (kuh-MYOO-nih-tee OR-guh-ny-zer)  Someone who helps people who live near each other come together over issues that are important to them.

**cultures** (KUL-churz)  The beliefs, practices, and arts of groups of people.

**cyberbullies** (SY-ber-bu-leez)  People who do hurtful or threatening things to other people using the Internet.

**discrimination** (dis-krih-muh-NAY-shun)  Treating a person badly or unfairly just because he or she is different.

**illegally** (ih-LEE-gul-ee)  Unlawfully.

**immigrated** (IH-muh-grayt-ed)  Moved to another country to live.

**migrant workers** (MY-grunt WERK-urz)  People who move from one place to another for work.

**population** (pop-yoo-LAY-shun)  A group of people living in the same place.

**scholarships** (SKAH-lur-ships)  Money given to people to pay for school.

**segregation** (seh-grih-GAY-shun)  The act of keeping people of one race, sex, or social class away from others.

**strikes** (STRYKS)  When workers refuse to work until changes are made.

**traditions** (truh-DIH-shunz)  Ways of doing things that have been passed down over time.

# Index

# Websites

Due to the changing nature of Internet links, PowerKids Press has developed an online list of websites related to the subject of this book. This site is updated regularly. Please use this link to access the list:

www.powerkidslinks.com/sbn/latino